THE NEW
PROPHET

Kevin MacNevin Clark

BALBOA.PRESS
A DIVISION OF HAY HOUSE

THE CAGE IS OPEN!

12-4-2020

Balboa Press books may be ordered through booksellers or by contacting:

Balboa Press
A Division of Hay House
1663 Liberty Drive
Bloomington, IN 47403
www.balboapress.com
844-682-1282

Because of the dynamic nature of the Internet, any web addresses or
links contained in this book may have changed since publication and
may no longer be valid. The views expressed in this work are solely those
of the author and do not necessarily reflect the views of the publisher,
and the publisher hereby disclaims any responsibility for them.

The author of this book does not dispense medical advice or prescribe the use
of any technique as a form of treatment for physical, emotional, or medical
problems without the advice of a physician, either directly or indirectly. The
intent of the author is only to offer information of a general nature to help
you in your quest for emotional and spiritual well-being. In the event you use
any of the information in this book for yourself, which is your constitutional
right, the author and the publisher assume no responsibility for your actions.

Any people depicted in stock imagery provided by Getty Images are
models, and such images are being used for illustrative purposes only.
Certain stock imagery © Getty Images.

Print information available on the last page.

ISBN: 978-1-9822-5415-5 (sc)
ISBN: 978-1-9822-5414-8 (hc)
ISBN: 978-1-9822-5419-3 (e)

Library of Congress Control Number: 2020916584

Balboa Press rev. date: 09/04/2020

Contents

In Appreciation

I would like to thank my beautiful family because *family first!* I thank my brave son, Abraham, the most emotionally intelligent five-year-old in this world. I thank my sweet daughter, Adelaide, a true artist who knows how to be silly. I thank my amazing daughter, Eve, for sharing her music with the world. I thank my badass wife, Allison, for granting me space and time, so I could put in the daily footwork to realize this book. I thank my brother for eagerly offering to help me in the editing process. I thank my father for believing in and being supportive of my vision. I thank my mother for never giving up on me; you have taught me that no one is a hopeless cause. I thank my best friend Aaron, who helped me bring this book to life with his generous support. I thank Rob for walking side by side with me on this path of seeking and doing the inside job these last eleven years. I thank God, who is the source of my creativity. I thank Carl, the very first therapist who meant anything to me. You saved my life, Carl, by giving me a safe space when I had none—and you were the first person I recall ever suggesting I write a book. I thank my therapist, Amanda; you remind me of all that I am capable of whether you know that or not. I thank all those who believe in me. I would not be where I am in this beautiful, messy journey without you all. I love you all, and yes, I mean ALL OF YOU, even you—actually *especially* you. *Thank you!*

Coming Home

There was a great counselor in Manasseh named Ishala. The story goes that he learned to heal his own wounds and shared that healing through his works. After his many years of giving back to others what he was once so freely given, Ishala felt tired knowing his final days were upon him.

He asked his children to take him to his old home so that he might spend his final days in the home he shared with his family, and where his beloved wife had passed away seven years past. His children attended to him as he lay in wait of his time coming. He smiled for he had no hard feelings.

He asked his son, Ezekiel, to go to the farmers market to get him jam, butter, and fresh bread. Now the people of Manasseh knew that Ishala had returned to end the journey of his "passing through." When he was at the market, Ezekiel was bombarded by requests from various townsfolk, pleading they be granted permission to come see his father to gather gems of his wisdom to take home to their own treasure troves. Ezekiel knew his father, perhaps better than anyone, and he knew his father would not want to be giving counsel on his last days. Throughout Ezekiel's childhood, Ishala would repeat his mantras of "Family first," and "In the end, what matters most is family." And so Ezekiel told the townsfolk he would go and speak to his father on the many topics the people asked about. Ezekiel promised to gather his father's wisdom and carry it back to the people. He always knew in his heart that this day would come, and so Ezekiel returned home and sat with his father as they shared toast and jam. In his wisdom, Ishala looked into Ezekiel's eyes and said, "Ask me, and I will answer." Ishala's smile lit up the room as a single silent tear fell from Ezekiel's face. And so began their last heart-to-heart. . .

Being Human

"Father, speak to me on what it means to be human."

Ishala smiled, pleased that his son began their conversation with such an expansive topic.

To be human is to be imperfect. To allow yourself to be human is to forgive.

Through that forgiveness, we extend grace to our neighbors. You see, we are all in this together, and all equal on a fundamental level.

Rumi said, "This *being human* is a guest house." We invite in whatever emotions arrive at our door; he called them guides from beyond.

When we practice this, we become increasingly intent on being better at feeling than feeling better.

Practice makes *better*, and we begin to both witness and experience the alignment of personality and soul.

"When do we know we have reached this perfect alignment?"

Ishala nodded at his son's question, for he knew there was danger in seeking perfection.

Perfectionism

Perfectionism is a weakness masquerading as a strength. It convinces man he is either right or wrong, leaving no room for the innumerable shades of gray, the tones of progress.

Perfectionism is the blade of grass missed by the mower that the landscaper obsesses over to the point that he forgets to water the garden.

The flowers wither and die, but damned if that blade of grass doesn't end up level with the rest of them.

Perfectionism is the storyteller of *never good enough*.

"I remember you working extensively with those who struggled with addictions. Tell me more of that work," Ezekiel requested.

Addiction

Addiction is not just the man with a bottle in his hand, or the woman with a needle in her arm; not just a man with a pipe in his mouth, or a woman with powder in her nose.

When addictions die, they are more often than not reincarnated as a different addiction made manifest.

Addiction is waking up in the middle of the night and polishing off a pint of ice cream.

Addiction is morning masturbation, causing you to be fifteen minutes late to work.

Addiction is *saying* you are staying late at work—and going to see a secret lover instead.

Addiction is answering work emails all weekend or allowing them to interrupt a vacation.

Addiction is checking your cell phone the moment you wake—looking for some likes or a message to validate who you think you are.

Addiction is a package of retail purchases on your doorstep more days than not.

It is the inability to walk away from the table before surrendering your paycheck or your child's college fund.

It is going back to the same snake to be bitten again and again—the poison coursing through your veins—an obsession screaming through every cell of your body—a hungry ghost haunting the corridors of your mind.

Addiction is a perpetual recovering of emotional discomfort.

Addiction is sedation and control.

Addiction feeds on secrets and loneliness.

Addiction is borne in isolation.

Addiction is not just cunning, baffling, and powerful—it is utterly merciless, infinitely patient, a liar, a cheat, and a thief. It wants to get you alone, and then it wants to kill you; sometimes slowly, and sometimes with a startling quickness—but not before stealing everything you hold dear first.

Addiction wipes life of meaning and takes the color out of sunsets.

Addiction will hurt all who come near it, for it does not only ravage its host. It ravages the host's family. It ravages the community, and it ravages the world.

Addiction takes!

The addicted mind serves substance.

The addicted mind screams in your ear for attention like a desperate child but will also whisper sweet words of seduction in your ear like the hot breath of a sensual partner in bed.

You see, addiction asks nicely but will also make demands like a desperate hostage taker. You are the hostage. You are also the one succumbing to the demands.

Addiction is tiresome for it is much work to wrestle demons day after day and night after night.

Day and night will lose definitive transitions when suffering this affliction.

Addiction is distraction. It is a sort of emotional misdirection wherein the con artist has you looking left while he steals your wallet on the right.

It is a perceptual sleight of hand wherein the con artist has you convinced you are holding onto your card only to discover nothing within your grasp.

This con artist isn't playing with a full deck. He is an illusionist; your eyes play tricks on you. Convinced you see something real, you walk blindly into oncoming traffic to be hurt at best and killed at worst.

Is addiction possession? Well, you're certainly owned.

To be free from addiction one must revolutionize one's thinking.

Recovery is the turned page, a new chapter. The page is blank, and as you hold pen in hand the page asks you to write a new story wherein you get to be the hero.

The story of recovery has innumerable new beginnings—a refreshing read after such a predictable plot—a tragedy—an obvious ending.

Life is a Choose-Your-Own-Adventure book. Many predestined endings. Free will chooses which way to go at every fork in prophecy.

"Please, Father, tell me more of recovery and its gifts." Ishala smiled and continued.

Recovery

Addiction is the language of "more." To recover is to "trust the process." In recovery, you recover *you*.

Addiction doesn't care the color of your skin, the job you have, or where you are from. It does not discriminate, and neither does recovery.

All-inclusive is the way of recovery—one of the many paths back to hope.

Recovery is sobriety—a soundness of mind.

Recovery is living in emotional balance. In recovery much is shared, for it is we who maintain it, and I who destroys it.

We examine our histories—and share them too.

Tears are shared and laughter too. We move out from under the encompassing shade that is the problem and into the ever expansive light that is the solution.

We are learning to love ourselves through this Spiritual kindergarten. Most take the elevator down then must use the steps to elevate themselves to new heights.

They return to a lush, vibrant world, a full spectrum of true colors; seeing life from this perspective of beauty, gratitude overwhelms them, and thus they live thanks, and give thanks.

Unity—Service—Recovery—trust God, clean house, help others. This is the way of those who occupy the rooms of recovery.

In recovery we go *through*—for we realize the only way out is *through*.

Again I tell you, we need not go through it alone. There is a host of people that will hold your hand when you're scared or need help when you cross the street.

There are many people who will pick you up if you fall, put you back on your feet and dust you off, offer words of encouragement, and point you in the right direction.

There are even times—your most trying of times when the people of recovery will come together and carry you when you are too weak.

You begin to see how God is channeled through a person's love, and so you lean into the process with a firm grasp on faith for stabilized footing.

Recovery is often misunderstood by those that walk the very path of it.

They *re-cover* their feelings with more vices, still choosing the belief of feeling better—getting high.

They eventually learn that if they don't deal with their issues, their issues will deal with them.

Pain demands to be felt, and like a creditor, pain will come to collect—with interest.

So instead take interest in feeling your feelings; that is why they're called feelings—remember—not *thinkings*.

Through this process of being with whatever arises, we participate in "The Inside Job" and uncover to discover our true Self. This is the Spiritual Awakening that the rooms of recovery promise.

Clear away the garbage that life and addiction have amassed atop you, and recover your Truth. I promise you will fall in love with it, and that you are *it*.

This is the Spiritual Awakening, and when you return Home reconnecting with your Soul identity—your sole purpose, recognizing Self as a child of God, it would be impossible to not be driven to carry and share this message to those still lost in the thick of the woods of addiction, the wilderness of Spiritual sickness.

Ezekiel was quiet, allowing himself a moment to digest his father's words. Finally, he spoke. "You always spoke of service, and you speak of it again today. Please tell me more about service, father, and what it means to you."

Ishala took a small bite of toast and breathed deeply. *The importance of service*, he thought.

Service

A cts of service let your Soul shine, your aura glow. You see, acts of service shine light into dark places illuminating the way back Home for others.

So let the light of Love move you, for even a kind smile serves your sister.

Service opens the door, never to earn thanks, but to fill the cup of his brother's heart, and in so doing his own cup overflows.

Giving for the sake of giving. This generosity of Spirit receives through giving.

Compassion is truly inexhaustible—it remains energized. Empathy must rest, though, for empathy is what makes us most human.

Compassion is what makes us most Divine.

"And service is impossible without community," Ishala continued. "Community is where you connect with your tribe, my son."

Ezekiel nodded, his eyes earnest in their curiosity. "Father, speak to me of community."

Community

They say it takes a village to raise a child, so be wise in choosing where you lay your head at night.

The need to belong is part of human experience; however, when this need speaks through desperation, we find ourselves in conflict with core values in our starvation for social support, our hunger for human connection. This is often the opportunity for gangs, militias, cults and the like.

We want friends and family so fiercely, we surrender our free-thinking minds, often scarring our personality.

Righteous community offers true understanding.

Righteous community shows up for you with no expectation of returned support.

Community will envelop you with love during times of trials, tribulation, and tragedy.

Community does not make demands of you; rather its message is one encouraging you to practice self-love and self-respect, for these are the chief traits of the self-governed person.

People still need people, so mindfully find your tribe.

Show me your friends, and I will show you your future. Anyone becomes a prophet abiding by this simple wisdom.

Connection, Friendship, & Unity

The mature man will always choose four quarters over one hundred pennies. They are easier to count on.

The immature man needs this change, sacrificing depth for the shallow surface of popularity. The immature man has lost connection with who he is.

Without such awareness and acceptance, he seeks the validation of many, rather than the counsel of few.

However, the strength of many can carry Higher Purpose much farther than the individual man.

Unity teaches us the power of *we* in contrast with the weakness of *me*.

With one eye a person can see, but with two eyes one can see everything that is before them.

When we form a circle holding hands we see the world in its entirety.

We—a word of immense power. Me—a word of significant limitations.

Ezekiel asked his father, "Is the 'me' what separates us all?"

Separation

Separation is the overcast sky. Separation is the darkness confusing the light that they are both parts of the same day.

Separation tells me I must safeguard what I have or it will be taken.

Separation sees differences and runs for the hills—fortifying fortresses to keep the sickness in.

Separation tells me God is in the sky though his children walk on earth.

It is the river that creates a mirage of division; the land on either side travels under the riverbed and meets beneath its waters. The river travels over the land. If a villager from one side of the river takes a drink from it, does not a villager on the other side of the river drink from the same water?

Both villagers stand under the same sun. Their skin may appear different, but the general design and overall purpose remain the same.

Do not focus on separation; return to unity. And unity may be gained through integration.

Integration

Integration is the spark of electricity that is felt when two hands shake.

Integration is making love and looking into one another's eyes to see your Self. Integration is feeling what we have fought to feel.

Integration restores the fractured psyche.

Integration gives you comfort in your skin again. Comfort left you in innocence; sometimes comfort left before a traumatic birth.

Integration is rebirth of intuition. Integration restores trust in the host. It merges ideas and shares core values. It is the jovial friend initiating the group hug.

It uses hindsight to develop insight. Through insight integration provides foresight.

Integration uses different farming tools to reap the full harvest.

It is when all pieces of the puzzle fit perfectly together, no edges forced into alignment. The pieces were always whole, though as you have been told, "The whole is greater than the sum of its parts."

Integration views the big picture. Separation cannot see the forest for the trees when its face is stuck against the bark.

Ezekiel looked puzzled. "Comfort left in innocence, father?"

Ishala nodded. "I speak of childhood, my son."

Inner Child

Everybody has one; though sometimes the adult has placed the child in time-out. That isn't parenting—not when the child has been left there for many years. This is neglect. Parenting involves nurturing—care-giving.

Your inner child just wants to play with you. A child always remembers fondly playing with mom and dad.

So don't walk through life forgetting this aspect of Self. Be silly and remember what it's like to be a child; stay silly to never forget—this is the way of the clever adult.

Some children get locked away and forgotten. The child grows sad; then the child becomes scared. Before too long you have an angry child screaming at the top of his little lungs.

Eventually the child becomes sick.

This is true sadness, and we see the evidence of this in the world we live in.

When you become reacquainted with your inner child, do not feel guilty for he has already forgiven you.

He remembers why you locked him up in the first place—to protect him, to keep the both of you alive.

Instead feel overjoyed, for the day has come where you can finally love yourself again.

Welcome him home with a hug and get to playing. You are strong enough to protect him, but you won't need to anymore.

That purpose has been served. Your best days are ahead of you yet; so live not in regret but cherish every moment enjoying the gift that is the aliveness of the Present.

Codependency

Codependency is when you and I become I.

When you are sad, I am sad; you must be happy for me to be happy, but when I am sad it doesn't mean you are sad; so I become unbalanced.

Boundaries are blurred and sometimes non-existent.

"Who would I be without you?" This is a question codependency asks in absolute uncertainty.

Codependency is a loss of Self through relationship, an enmeshment of identity. Self-worth tied up with relational success.

The codependent relationship is to build your house on sand—the foundation unstable much like infatuation.

Though much of life is taking down walls, some of it is spent in building them. The stone edgers placed around your garden keep the nurturing soil in— ensuring the needs of the flower are met, so that it may bloom in its season of growth.

Boundaries are created with the spoken word and edified by the voice of confidence.

Vulnerability & Intimacy

I return to my certain self by sharing my uncertainties.

We take off our armor because though it protects us from hurt, we cannot be held while wearing it.

Walls come up in relationships. To be vulnerable is to speak your truth, to show up raw and real. We stand naked uncomfortably letting all eyes fall upon our skin so that we may be comfortable in that very skin we are in.

Intimacy—Is there such a thing as too close for comfort?

Not between people if the people are truly comfortable in the skin they're in. That is why some say, "Into me I see." It is the optimal way to take advantage of this house of mirrors we are living in.

One school of thought is that everyone we meet in our dreams is really ourselves—a piece of our unconscious mind. To enter a dream lucidly with this understanding, we realize we are all part of the collective Consciousness.

Do we dream peacefully? Or do we toss and turn terrorized by our unmet selves?

So it is when one becomes emotionally intimate with one's Self that forgiveness transforms their pain into love, an organic alchemy of the soul.

We realize the monsters under our bed are only monsters in our head; and leaving irrational fears behind, we merge energy with those around us.

We see the Good in our neighbor. We see the God in our lover. We live in Spiritual experience, synchronized with the world.

This is authentic intimacy. This is to feel safe and at home wherever you go, so consider carefully what you feed your mind, as it has a way of infecting your consciousness.

Input equals output. This simple equation will keep the doors of your home open and inviting, but be ever vigilant for it can also bar your doors—locking you in and the world out. Nothing seems safe. This is Spiritual homelessness.

Balance

Balance is the conscious connected breath—measured with each exhale matching its inhale.

The path to balance often looks chaotic, and when you arrive at such a place, a certain amount of vigilance and focus, coupled with need and intention, are necessary to stay in the middle of the wide road.

As you move toward the sides, away from smooth center, the ground becomes coarse, then jagged; potholes and deep cracks start to form ruts as the pavement crumbles away to either side into the ditch there.

If one does stumble, slip, and fall over the edge of these pits, there is but one way out: extending a hand upward. *One must ask for help.* Such a man needs help from something above him.

Nature restores balance. Man cannot take from the earth without consent. There are consequences to such rapacious actions. This is called homeostasis, necessary to keep any living system functioning effectively.

So be mindful—are you making time to do what you love?
Making time for work? Making time for friendship? For family?
Making time for solitude—giving yourself the space of Presence?

The balanced person says yes.

Structure

All structures are moveable. Some foundations last longer, but all is temporary structure.

We need order for this play of forms, do we not? What is a skyscraper without its framework?

A skyscraper. Let us play with this word; something that reaches farther than it really should and challenges the heavens. Blemishes itself upon earth's atmosphere. Corporate structures, symbols of the pollutants that threaten Mother Nature.

Humanity. We steal from our own Mother's purse. Even if we all only steal five dollars, we still leave a broken home, a crumbling structure for the next dweller with much work needed to rebuild.

To rebuild trust—trust that we will do no harm to our own family. This is a family disease.

There are structures where there should be fluidity or even open spaces—emptiness—where true creation is born.

There is chaos where we need order. Mother Nature, she enforces order, but she wants to trust her children again.

Trust them that she can again leave her purse open, and the disciplined child, living within his own walls of integrity, does not cave inward like an avalanche of avarice, addiction, and impulsivity.

You see, we humans need structure; we crave it at an unconscious level, but the Conscious man needeth not structure. He has awakened to the eternal wellspring of the Universe and walks in alignment with the floetry of God.

Routine

Does the Spiritual man keep routine?

Yes, routine is different than structure. To walk a tightrope, you walk a straight line. When you're parenting yourself and working without a net, you watch your breath but never hold it.

In and out you breathe with the tides. Kneeling when in pain, the Spiritual man returns to the ground—leaning in to ask his Mother for safety. Looking upward, he asks his Father for a sign, for direction.

Go back to the basics with the slogans, "Easy Does It, But Do It!" and "First Things First,"—Walk in the direction of your Father's Kingdom and the way will be laid out in front of you.

Routine is the map etched into your mind once it has been buried in your heart. The daily practice of putting one foot in front of the other is the easiest way Home. Practice makes *better*, better makes *easier*. Practice is repetition. Reinforcement of our own footwork, whether it be fancy or basic.

Trust is the well-trodden path. We learn to trust in ourselves again—lean into our own hearts. As I lean into my heart, I lean into *her* heart. Together the children of love will lead with their hearts, sharing that heart's map with the rest of the world.

So you see, it is highly important we determine which walls come down, and which walls we erect in the remodeling of our metaphysical structure.

What do we want to keep out? I leave my shades open to let the light in. I leave the windows open, so I can hear the trickling of running water—the soothing sound of serenity. Open—so I can listen to the birds sing me songs of serendipity. Each chirp reminds me I have awoken to a new day and am hungry; so I must eat.

Being a creature of habit—it is to be stressed how dangerous habits can be too. How unhealthy it can be to be stuck in routine of ill repute. How toxic the structures of ego can be! Obsessive— always obsessive—obsessively locking doors because of fear.

The man that always keeps his door locked is not permitting his child to run free and roam the great outdoors!

"No! I keep the door locked to keep you safe!" he bellows at his child who is shrinking back into the corner, shaking like a leaf. This child, having never experienced true freedom, will pass this fear onto others.

Ego, the key that locks the door, is the great skeleton key. It is the same key we used to keep our closets locked. That is why we call it a skeleton key. As we turn the lock of judgment, the bolt of shame moves into place—barricading Self from any visitors.

Our children forget to play. They forget the world. They forget how to connect through our similarities to celebrate our differences. The world gets smaller every day.

It is time to melt these keys down; turn them to art, share the art with our neighbors.

It is time to return to trust, to let go of structures of fear and anger, and to build instead structures of faith and Love.

Live in this structure and throw a party. Be sure to invite all children.

Fear

Fear, what a strange thread woven throughout the tapestry of our existence.

When I feel such corrosion, I project anger onto my reality.

Fear whispers in your ears. Fear speaks with a sweet tongue, spreading its lies for control.

Fear tells the follower that to follow fear is to have control, but this sweet-tongued manipulation is to gain control of you!

For from fear all malice is born. Fear births many hurts: resentment, judgment, greed, lust, shame. Ah yes, shame is the name of the game.

Once fear has you eating from the shame plate, he's got his grip closing around your jugular like a constrictor.

Fear attaches itself to the host, starving the heart of Love; screaming in your ears inexhaustibly, with the goal of banishing your childlike faith.

When fear has you, there is never enough. When fear has you, you will get hurt. When fear has you, you will fail. Or better yet, you will succeed, but still be led to ruin.

Yes, fear has you convinced you are unloved and unworthy of it.

This is when fear has its roots deeply embedded in you. Your soul is tangled up in egoic silliness. What if you can't get back Home?

You've gotten so spun around, you lose sense of direction; so guarded, arms tight to chest for protection—refusing to let Love in, because what if it hurts you?

That Love can hurt is the biggest lie of all. *Love can do no wrong.* Again I tell you, Love can do no wrong.

Fear can have you on the run. Fear can make you take up arms. Fear can paralyze you. Yes, you are stuck when struck by fear—but what most don't see is the bludgeoning done between your ears.

You think you wrestle demons, but the fight you have is with your little self. You run *to* something when you're running *away from* something. You must open your arms.

This scared child needs a hug. He wants you to hold his hand when crossing the street. He needs to feel safe.

The mirage of fear has divided man. A mirage can only divide when we believe the lie. The connection has never been stronger, for even as I tell you this, you briefly see through the fog.

Fear lives in the future but was born in the past, and is never in the here-and-now. Not the fear we are talking about, the one between your ears with a brain as its plaything, like a cat batting a ball of yarn.

Imagination can be stifled by fears. What if you waste your time? What if you waste your time? There is irony in the clarity of the repetitive nature of fear.

Fear is always begging you to be rigid in thought—no free form. If you color outside the lines you will not be accepted.

"What if there is not enough time?" the past asks the future. The Present reminds us that the only time is *now* and there is always enough now to go around for it is everywhere at all times.

Now is eternal, ever changing, always constant. Presence is packed with peace and joy, but first cobwebs of fear must be cleared away.

Vision restored, Love is born. Courage is fear walking. Courage is fear that has said its prayers. Courage is prayer without ceasing. Courage is not a calm force—but damn is it energized. It packs a punch.

"Is it true that it is fear that breeds hate?" Ezekiel inquired.

Hate

Hate—it consumes energy, for it is a fire that always needs feeding 'til not one tree remains standing in the forest.

You see, this fire always wants more energy, bigger flames. The damage spreads across the land. It matters not if the hate is for disease or a person.

Sure if the fire burns for disease or an institution, the fire starter will feel better about themselves. This is no better than if the fire is lit for another person. But the worst burning hatred is hatred of self.

It sears deep, and because it feeds itself, it spreads wildly, doing devastating damage with an immediacy that sends shudders through my bones.

The point is that hate is born in resentment. We drink the poison, and the only person killed is ourselves—usually dying an agonizingly slow death.

The fires of hatred and the poisons of resentment can slowly sicken the body of *We*. The death incurred wounds the Spirit.

The wind of the Spirit retreats, refusing to fan the flames; the mouth of God spits out the poison, rejecting the vile taste.

Hate and resentment leave mankind lost, confused, enshrouded in darkness. Mankind fumbles around on the ground frantically searching for the eyes they believe have gone missing. Dumb to the reality that the only thing that needs to be done is to take a deep breath. Be still. Open your eyes, and look within.

Looking within will neutralize the poison. Search with your heart and quench the fire's thirst with the water of a thousand tears. For just like you and me, hatred often mistakes thirst for hunger, and instead of seeking simple hydration, hatred becomes morbidly obese.

Love

When Love looked in the mirror, she saw herself, and in that moment she saw everyone else.

Love doesn't keep score and can do no wrong.

Love shows up as a gift from God that many fear to open.

What if my gift makes me into something I am not? What if I lose it? What if I break it? What if she breaks me?

Love heals. She connects. She meets pain smiling in kindness. Love gives pain a hug. She does not judge. Love cares not what you believe, what color your skin is, or how much money you make.

Love is the answer to problems seeming unsolvable.

She walks tall and confident, bringing men to their needs in blissful servitude. She gives us presents with her Presence alone. It has been said that *all you need is Love*.

She is a universal language spoken from the heart, and has been sung of countless times in another universal language—*music*.

Love dissolves hate like an acid that, while painful in its process, is also blissful. Corrosion of the heart falls away, liberating the man and freeing his child. She is playful.

Mother Love is naturally nurturing, holding the world like a newborn baby, gently rocking it to sleep when he cries. She kisses his wounds as though he is a toddler who has fallen and scraped his knee in too much of a rush as he runs for the door. "Patience," she whispers in her amiable tone.

Love's voice is harmony—its string your inner power chord. Love is a major chord progression that can vibe in any song.

Love is never fearful. Love is curious instead. She is less likely to ask why, and more likely to warmly shrug her feminine shoulders, and say, "Why not?"

Though Love is the Divine feminine and gorgeous, so easy on the eyes, expanding pupils in excitatory dilation, she is in no way weak. She is the strongest power. When the love of power is transformed by and to the power of Love, ever present peace will greet you smiling.

Love's currency spends anywhere.

She is the dog running up to lick your face after a hard day of work. She is the deepest laughter connecting two souls. Love is the purifying tears healing cynicism, returning aged wounds to innocence.

Love is your inner sense. She will never mislead you, so follow her; follow her every footstep if at all possible. March to the beat of her drum, and let her carry you when you have exhausted all other resources and can travel no further.

Love is the river that flows back to the ocean Eternal. Love is a mysterious force flowing over jagged rocks, wearing them smooth.

Love is a mystical pool of reflection that when looking into it with perfect stillness, you see yourself. You see her. You see Love. Your body buzzes with the electricity of ancient knowing. It does not matter what you believe, it matters what you *know*.

Love is not romance in the sense many think. It is not jealous. It is constant and abundant like the air in your open lungs, filling you with the very breath of Life. There is no shortage.

Smiling at your neighbor to your left takes none away from you sharing that same smile with your neighbor to the right.

Love shares the sugar with no expectation of return. Her sweetness is clean.

Love is inexhaustible. Compassion fatigue is a myth. Always keep your well full and you will always have water on hand. You nor anyone else will go to sleep with a parched throat.

The wetness that is Love splashes warmly in erotic abundance. Orgasmic elation, heavenly Love turns an entire sexual experience into an epic of an orgasm.

Love will take you to new heights, but if you get fixated on looking down you will fall to hurt.

No, my friend, look deeply into her eyes and fall in. Fall in Love to her safety. She is the safe place of a mother's embrace.

When two children enlivened by adoration run up to hug their father after his long day of work, there is a cosmic chemical reaction, alchemy. This is the gold of life. Amber energy that with precision intention can spread like wildfire into the heart of every man, woman, and child.

Not all know Love. She knows all though; her memory like that of an elephant. She never forgets. The forgetful father passes his sins down to his son.

And so I ask you to ask the parents of Manasseh, what are you teaching your children? Do they play outdoors connected with others and their Mother's Love? Or do they sit inside alone? Disconnected by their screens? Learning to fear anything and everything unknown? Do they run from discomfort without even moving?

"I will ask them, father." But Ezekiel looked concerned, his brow furrowed in thought.

"What troubles you, Ezekiel?" asked Ishala.

"You spoke of shame, and its power."

Ishala looked out the window and nodded. "Of course. Let us discuss guilt, and shame."

Guilt & Shame

Guilt is the pain a child feels when he touches a stove. Shame is leaving the hand in place to burn and burn.

Guilt is the feeling you get from stealing five dollars from your mother's purse. Shame tells you, "You are a thief!" Shame reminds you, "You did something bad." Shame continues to whisper so long as you'll listen, *"You are something bad."*

Shame is a storyteller, and she tells tall tales that keep you feeling low.

Guilt can motivate one who cheats to be faithful. Shame will motivate that same person to do it again . . . and again . . . and again.

Shame speaks sharply: "You are shit, and therefore deserve shit treatment."

Guilt is the invisible slap to the face leaving it reddened—flushed. Shame is the heavy bag of meaningless boulders we've let ourselves be convinced we must carry 'til we collapse. Its weight causing our spine to curve, fixing our gaze upon our own feet. How can a man have a vision for what lies ahead when he is forever looking down upon himself?

This lack of foresight leads to walking in circles. The man becomes lost. He becomes sick and tired, never reaching a resting point.

Guilt can wake you up. Shame can put you to sleep.

The ashamed one may feel guilt even when he has committed no wrong.

Shame is gangrene of the soul, eating away at your Truth.

The guilty one will serve his sentence and be done with it. The ashamed one is wrongly convicted and sentenced to life imprisonment. He is both the judge and jury, and ultimately will be the executioner if he cannot forgive, stop walking in circles, and walk the straight path.

The ashamed man must empty his backpack of the boulders, usually dropping a few rocks here, a few rocks there. His circle of insanity gets bigger.

It begins to really seem like he is going somewhere in life! Only to return to the place where he began stacking his rocks.

Not until the last pebble of shame is removed from his boot, his shoes taken off, barefoot and vulnerable, grounded and strengthened, he finds his way Home.

Ezekiel felt the importance of his father's words. "So this is forgiveness?"

"This is one way in which forgiveness may look. But there is more we can say on the matter," Ishala continued.

Forgiveness

To release a grudge is to turn loose a pebble. But what of the unforgivable? How to forgive the sickest of souls—and sometimes you may be at this point—requires determination, and intention.

The artistry of forgiveness requires a chisel. For the unforgivable is the massive stone rolled in front of the tomb of your heart.

Forgiveness of another will unchain both you and your brother. Free yourself to be yourself. For hurt people *hurt* people, so understand the pain you have suffered is resultant of the pain *they* suffered.

Forgiving is not forgetting but rather an integration and release of the negative charge embedded in the body, in charge of the mind. No man shackled with resentment is a free thinker. Instead, it rents space in his head for free, holding a reservation for no one at all really.

Forgiveness is a two-way street. As I forgive you, I forgive *me*. As I forgive me, I forgive you. Releasing the poison of past hurts gives birth to the sweetest song that will go unsung should the tongue remain wrapped up in malice or should the voice be trampled by trauma that goes unhealed.

Trauma is the hurt that is carried from past lives to the skin you're in.

Resentment

If someone hands you a bag of dog feces, why carry it around when you didn't have to pick it up in the first place?

Live life carrying other people's messes and your hands become full, unable to receive gifts.

The stench—you become accustomed to it. You try to make new friends or are attracted to a new lover, but are left wondering why no one wants to be around you.

"Why do they abandon me?" you cry out in self-pity.

Resentment locks you into loneliness, for no one wants to attend the pity party.

Self-Pity

So what now of self-pity?

You've heard the adage, "Poor me, poor me. . . . Pour me a drink!" Such is the nature of self-pity.

It sits in loneliness, hanging paintings on the wall of this rut.

It grows comfortable like a mold that creeps in the dark. Self-pity will not thrive in the light of day.

Self-pity spits in the face of responsibility—the spattered saliva a hundred excuses.

Responsibility

Your ability to respond determines your capacity for responsibilities.

Know that the man who manages much is well acquainted with the gift of pause.

He knows the importance of taking a breath before taking an action.

Responsibility asks questions and lives in Truth. It does not budge when the weight of authority pushes in persuasion to break bond with integrity. We've all heard that with great power comes great responsibility.

The immature man runs from responsibility; not wanting to part ways with his good buddy reactivity. "I get to do what I want when I want, and if I want it right now, I will make it mine," speaks such egoic minds.

Deluded—for he has convinced himself the rusty shackles he wears are fine jewelry. He does not pause to take stock of the harm he does himself, which as we know, by connectivity, means he does everyone else.

For how can a man driven by the charge of impulse be in charge of his own experience? No such thing is possible.

The responsible man lives by the code of intention, remaining teachable, for he knows not who will be his next teacher. He is taught by the child having a temper tantrum. He is taught by the resentful lover. He is taught by the power-hungry employer. He is taught by the death of his father. He is taught by the falling of his tears.

Responsibility learns through reflection of its fears.

Faith

True faith is unbreakable. It remains steadfast through human doubt.

Faith knows. Doubt thinks.

Faith takes action and is decisive. Doubt procrastinates for fear of making the wrong choice.

Faith is kinetic energy. Doubt is potential energy paralyzed.

Faith trusts. Doubt lies.

Faith is an oak tree. Beginning as an acorn, sprouting to a sapling, and over time becoming stronger, and one day—immovable.

Self-Doubt

Self-doubt is a web that covers your confidence in its sticky trappings.

Self-doubt starts sentences with words such as, "I think."

Self-doubt ends sentences with statements such as, "or something like that." Self-doubt turns statements into questions.

Seeking validation, self-doubt shrinks with a slouched posture and averted gaze.

Self-doubt is the rod in the spokes of the wheel of decision-making.

Self-doubt fears to show its face—fears to admit its identity.

Self-doubt will often wear a mask of confidence, though the mask is transparent allowing the face beneath, flushed with insecurity, to be seen by any who pay attention.

The self-centeredness of codependency searches the mind, begging the question: what have I done wrong!?

Be impeccable with your word. Say what you mean and mean what you say. Self-doubt will forever guard you from success.

If you don't use your voice, you lose your voice. Use your voice. This is the mark of self-esteem.

Self-Worth

What is self-worth?

For what it is worth all selves have it, but often it is depleted through defective conditioning and other hurts of living.

Like a plant needing nurturing, we must water the inherent value that is in us all. This plant can thrive with the proper care.

The green thumb of compassion bears a fruitful harvest, where many can eat from such a garden.

A neglected plant may wither and even get sick with disease, but with tender loving care by the hand of an expert gardener, even a deathly-ill plant can be rejuvenated and again shimmer with the green energy of life.

So watch your words with others, asking yourself, "Do my words give or do they take?"

Take this advice I give you to your heart of hearts. Be generous to your innermost Being and grow your Self. Be wary of cutting down your innermost Being and be left with little self. Know Self—no self.

Again I tell you, all Selves have worth in the hands of the Loving Gardener.

Relationships

Toxic relationships—in the toxic relationship one may lose their voice one of two ways.

One way is to forget how—your speech disempowered.

The other is to exhaust one's vocal chords through fits of screaming.

In healthy relationship each partner's voice meets in harmony for the chorus, but still gives the other space to sing their own solo. Lovers are encouraged to write their own song. Echoes the words—*Love Can Do No Wrong*.

Relationships involve sacrifice balanced with self-care.

Self-Care

What is self-care?

Self-care is action and self-care is rest.

When you give to yourself, you care for others.

Self-care is a massage for your body, a favorite book for your mind, time spent with a loved one for your Soul.

Self-care is the mindful breath you take when lightning strikes all around you.

Self-care is the pause you give yourself before lashing out cruelly with your tongue.

Self-care is water on the body.

Self-care is strengthening muscles through training.

Self-care is the stretch you take to bookend your exercise routines.

Self-care is a comedy show, as it is as much a vibrant laugh as it is a mournful cry.

Self-care is to live with integrity. Yes means yes. No means no. Remaining true to who you really are: this, my friend, is the best care you can show to Self.

Self

What is Self?

Self is your highest level of consciousness—your Truth and connection to the rest of the Universe.

It will mirror the man—his personality—but only in authenticity when the man is awake to Self, the Self who has always been there, waiting for renewed relationship.

Self guides you like a father, nurtures you like a mother, and plays with you like a child.

No self is to know Self. The illusion must be vanished with intention to open up this channel.

I say illusion because the channel is open—already in waiting. The Self is merely obstructed by mistaken beliefs and old ideas.

Self is incarcerated by an identity shaped by fear.

When we make Self wear too many masks for too many nights, daylight will not shine on the face of Self, for his face was long forgotten in this state of perpetual dream.

Self begins to sink to the depths, weighed down by perceived separation.

Do not be confused. Listen when I say, this man *you* show up as, whether it be your Truth or not, is the truth you show to the world.

Self asks you to examine your beliefs. Are they of service to me and others?

The Self begs the question, "What do you really know?" To get this answer one must cultivate peace of mind.

Self watches self through the window pane of awareness. When self has exhausted himself, self opens the window, for remember, stillness speaks and winds bring in new ideas.

Self is never in inner conflict. If a fight exists between happy and right, this is not Self. Self has nothing to prove, resting in absolute Truth.

Self is the shining Sun. He shines, no matter the weather. Gray clouds may hang in the sky, rain may pound down to the earth, but he is still there—his fire eternal and patient.

The Self in you is not so different from the Self in your brother, as the finger and thumb both belong to the same hand.

Remember, separation is the enemy of your neighborhood. It is the lie.

"Tell me more of the dangers of not telling yourself the truth," Ezekiel queried.

Denial

Denial is the blind spot for the prophet.

When reality overwhelms the eyes, we find ways to learn not to see.

Sometimes one's field of vision is obscured by so many distractions. We are unable to find the problem requiring acceptance. This is the easiest denial to reverse, for when there is a seer, he simply shows his friend what he would benefit from finding.

The second level of denial is when we take our problem and hide it in that drawer we rarely open. "Out of sight, out of mind," we think, and we are correct.

Only someone insane would believe that if they don't look at their bald spot, they remain with a full head of hair.

The third level is when that same person believes their comb-over means they are not bald.

And the fourth level is when they look straight at that same bald spot and actually see hair!

Denial becomes lunacy as the mind sinks into its depths.

Sadness

The river of tears that must flow back to the ocean. We mustn't dam it up, lest we create an unwanted reservoir of depression.

This water begins to build along the shoreline, re-shaping what was meant to be. Holding back such tears creates an emotional stuck point.

Eventually that dam will need to come down, whether that act is accomplished through thoughtful intention, or whether it simply bursts, flooding the earth around it, uprooting the very nature of how neat we wanted our shoreline to appear.

So cry an ugly one now and later save face through genuine *being* rather than by wearing a mask of forced positivity.

Sadness exists for a reason. The river of tears is meant to flow in one direction; such is the easier softer way. Constructing levees to alter the flow of nature's response to pain again requires so much energy.

Sadness remains buried in every Soul until the inside job is complete. Men run from sadness mistaking a gift for a curse.

Sadness is the hurt of healing. When denied entry at the doorway, sadness sets up camp on man's front porch; so the man hides in his house waiting for his unwelcome guest to depart

But before too long a depression fills the home. The man inside is now cut off from all he loves in life, isolated and detached.

The depressed man peers out his window and sees sadness sitting there slouched and seated waiting on the porch. He now thinks that if he lets him in he will never leave. Depression becomes paranoia.

When he finally opens the door and addresses this unwanted visitor, he shouts, "Well, what is it? What do you want from me?"

Sadness replies, "It is not what I want to take from you, it is what I want to give to you."

Looking bewildered the depressed man stands there while sadness envelops him in a hug. His home finally cleansed with tears, happiness and joy rush over to be with the man again. "We missed you," they say, smiling warmly.

In this story your heart is the house, and for it to be full its door must remain open.

Happiness

Happiness is a choice you have heard. It is an inner state achieved only through presence.

Journey consciousness finds happiness in the here and now. Destination consciousness chases it forever, never to find it.

Never reaching his intended destination, the man becomes discouraged, developing a negative worldview, enlisting pessimism, oft under the guise of realism.

So happiness is a choice. By choosing it in this moment, I dwell in optimism. This is no act. Happiness is not an act in its true form.

Happiness smiles inwardly as it beams outwardly.

Again I emphasize, happiness is found in This Present Moment. There is no *if-then* to be happy. *If* may be the biggest word in life but *ifs* and *thens* can stand in the way of our happiness much like the dam stands before our sadness.

Am I resting in the here and now, or am I living behind the dam? Am I convincing myself the ocean is around the next bend? Am

I going with the flow? Can't I see that the river is as much the ocean as the tear that streams down the cheek?

Be like water, for it has its own wisdom. And it remembers. It remembers everything.

Let the stream of Consciousness flow. It comes from the Ocean, and it goes back to the Ocean. It *is* the Ocean. When a stream strays too far off course, it must close its eyes and remember; for when I close my eyes I see.

Who among us knows what lies beneath the surface and its uncharted depths? Is there a secret city? The Ocean knows of course, so get with the merging to understand your depths.

"But there is so much pain in this world, father. How do we prevent ourselves from being overwhelmed by all of it?"

"You are speaking of trauma, my son." Ishala continued.

Trauma

Trauma is the wound that can be seen in the eyes of the hurting. It is written on her face, her eyes usually cast downward. She is scared of touch, and scarred by it too.

You see, some wounds remain open—their hurt the same as the day they were injured, even many years later. Their pain does not change with the seasons, whereas other injuries of the heart and mind result in scar tissue—numb to the touch—sensations deadened.

Both wounds need healing so she can feel the rest of her body. Each trauma fractures psyche—the mending a delicate process that requires a steady hand, a skilled mind, and an open heart.

She must relive her painful past in a safe space with borrowed strength so that she may stand tall and free. Hurts heal in hope.

Trauma is the past setting your skin on fire in the present.

The pain stored in the body, sometimes the hurt walk in their sleep, detached from that very body to avoid the burn of its hot flames.

Healing is the cool water, the body of the hurt immersed within it. When the healed rest their eyes, they sleep in peace. No more wars wage in their heads. It is the deep breath awakening to the here and now. Permission granted to return to the sensations of the body. Dwelling in a safe place, you have arrived back Home.

Healing is found in the sound of music, so use it. Listen and receive.

It is true that "The whole is greater than the sum of its parts," so to make a Self whole again, you must honor and work with each part—the hidden and hurt, the sentry standing guard to control and patrol the perimeter, and the emergency response team waiting for the worst.

Harmonize the band members, have them work in concert with one another to sing the songs of Self—the sound produced will be a joyful one! This joy feeds the Self *hope*.

Hope & Joy

J oy is ever present and can be experienced by the identification and removal of who we are not. Joy abides in the Present Moment.

Joy cannot be experienced by the man who runs from hurt. To dodge pain is to dodge joy. Numb is numb.

But what then is Hope? Hope is the rainbow after the storm. Hope is the bird who has not yet used its wings, for when it flies its song is faith.

Hope walks through the fire, while faith leaps over the flames. Hope is the look before you leap, trusting you will land on your feet. Faith *leaps*.

Hope is a vision of tomorrow that rests in today.

Hope is something to hold onto when all else is out of reach, leaving you with an otherwise empty grasp.

Hope has peace in the knowing that as surely as the sun sets ushering in the night, the light of day returns at dawn.

"We need more hope and joy in this world father," Ezekiel said, contemplatively.

Ishala let out a deep sigh and continued.

Diversity & Collective Trauma

Different skin colors are so important for awakening. It is not that we should see without color. A world in grayscale is a bleak existence indeed. But to appreciate the many nuances of the prism that is multicultural intimacy is to live in Love.

Shall we exist or *live*? We cannot deny the truth. The days of deluded thinking come to a screeching stop as the age of ego crumbles.

Yes, we certainly need a movement. I empathize with the rage of the trauma born from the blood shed on this very soil, those deeply embedded hurts, passed down generation to generation.

I know with absolute certainty that hurt people *hurt* people, which only means more hurting, more re-traumatizing.

To move past a collective trauma we must march onward, but before we can move forward together we must individually allow ourselves to feel the collective pain—the fear, the anger, and ultimately the sadness, that many of us have worked so hard to *not* see.

After the hurt is released from the collective body, we can truly march forward into tomorrow on a united front. We can all lead with Love.

Remember who you are!

Healing

More about healing.

Some wounds cut deeper than others. Some wounds scar the Soul.

Like a scarred liver, it becomes more and more difficult to show up for its work. This is a slow Soul death.

This sort of healing requires corrective surgery, a skilled hand guided by God Himself. It is a painful process—a re-opening of the wounds.

Though the pain can be excruciating, the process is much more primitive and once undertaken the disability of the Soul begins to lift.

Therapy

What is therapy?

It is said it is a series of getting lost and finding yourself.

When healing trauma, if the body is hot—dive headfirst into the pool and begin swimming, but, if the body is cold, wade into the water—feet first. When you near the depths, it is time to swim.

For some wounds will turn the body numb, whereas some wounds set sensation afire.

In therapy, a safe place must be provided. Ask permission before examining wounds.

True healing addresses the wound itself, though often symptoms of the hurt must be treated first to determine its origin.

Two tools you must have are empathy and compassion, but do not use pliers when the job is calling for a drill.

The therapist shows the person seeking counsel where the weak spots in his walls are, and helps that person develop the strength necessary to break down those very walls, for they must come down from the *inside*.

The therapist, by invitation, travels with his client into the darkest places of the mind, shining a light and providing a map, so that the client can himself find his way out of the darkness.

Therapy is an art; the art of piecing back together pottery that has been shattered, in some cases into many minuscule fragments—each shard beautiful but razor sharp. The vase must be restored in order to hold flowers again.

The skilled therapist is a mind mechanic; he knows which gears perform what functions, and there is an assortment of tools for different repairs.

The greatest tool is no tool at all, it is simple human connection—empathy. It is one human being creating space for the other in being human.

The intuitive counselor is a blindfolded archer. As a blindfolded archer I shoot confidently, I *sense* the bullseye before releasing the arrow from the bow. I let go, surrendering to the creative flow of the Universe, the arrowhead pulled by Divine Guidance.

I take off my blindfold in time to see the target hit. I watch the unraveling of awakening from the inside out, the physical jolt, as the somatic system integrates the hidden memory.

Cognition engines out of use fire up, and as they do, you see shock in the face of the target—bewilderment. They begin their feeble attempt to explain that for which words will not suffice. Before too much easily understood can be spoken, enter the waterworks.

True beauty is when they set their weapons to the side and with defenses fully down, the floodgates of suppressed pain open up. An exodus of tears flows, sobbing—feeling for healing.

Their inner child is acknowledged, truly seen, and given safe passage to join them in the Present Moment.

This is the healing magic, the "wizard shit" of intuitive counseling. The intuitive counselor teaches the student through the mastery of the Present Moment.

Presence

The Present Moment is the only moment that exists. The mental body fights this reality, arguing how can the past not exist? And the future? This is nonsense, it says, and in engagement of this argument we continue to forfeit Presence.

Distraction is to *do*. Presence is to *be*. Distractions enter the arena of creativity.

What exactly is Presence? Presence is living as a channel—calling upon the power of this Moment.

Presence is everywhere at once and all at the same time. The time is now and that is all that exists. Here, all else is illusory.

The past is a doorway, but we cannot walk through it. We look into it from the Present. Careful, though, for to stare into it too longingly is to lose awareness of the Great Reality.

From the Present we see through the third eye into possibilities of what is to come; though stare not into it with fixated attention, for you will miss the gift of Being.

Presence is the energy that makes up the totality of us all. When you meet the Present man you say, "Such powerful Presence." His energy is felt—a perception which cannot be denied, even by the sleepwalker.

The Present man dreams while awake, experiences dripping with surrealism.

Presence is the bird that finally left the open cage to fly free.

And so it is that even when lost in thought to the point of bated breath and vision fogged in fear, the aliveness of Presence is present.

Begin to watch your thoughts instead of *being* your thoughts.

Presence asks of you but one thing: *be where your feet are.* To ground yourself, take off your shoes and stand in the grass.

"There is much peace in presence," Ezekiel stated, speaking his thoughts aloud.

Serenity

Serenity is the full glass of water that spills not a drop in the midst of the earth quaking. It is a powerful stillness encompassed by the glass of acceptance.

The serene person not only meets life where *it* is, he meets others where *they* are. And last but certainly not least, he meets himself where he is.

There is an acute awareness of what he can and cannot change. The serene man does not attempt to manipulate such Universal Law.

Peaceful, he knows his piece, living in the wisdom of adjusting his own attitude and actions to what *is*, rather than trying to force it to be what he wants it to be.

Ezekiel asked, "To adjust one's attitude to what is, is this what it takes to cultivate an 'attitude of gratitude'?"

Gratitude

Gratitude is the law of abundance.

To train the mind to believe in ample appreciation is to see all that you have. You must believe it to see it; and at a starting point see it to believe it.

Gratitude feeds itself and when the belly gets full it gives birth to puppies, and its puppies produce more pups. This is the law of abundance. It never wants what it does not have, because it *does* want everything it already has.

It is said that a grateful heart knows no conceit, that you cannot be grateful and hateful simultaneously.

Gratitude lets you fall in love with life. We fiercely protect that which we fall in love with.

Gratitude teaches the student to stay out of his own way. Student becomes master as his own way comes into alignment with Yahweh.

The grateful person gives thanks in all things, generous even in their appreciation for their struggles. Trials and tribulations open doors for lessons, and lessons transform into blessings.

Gratitude grounds you in the stillness that is the Present Moment, which some call the peace that surpasses all human understanding.

Therefore it never fights; it casually walks the pathway of acceptance.

Its vision is that of a child's—widened with the fullness of awe and wonderment.

It is also said that the man with no shoes complains until he meets the man with no feet, so when twisted with complaint, step outside of yourself and always remember that you do not *have* to, you *get* to.

"And what of those who struggle to find meaning in what they are given to do? What do you know of purpose, father?"

Purpose

A life without purpose is not any kind of life at all. It is a hollow existence.

The man without it aimlessly wanders through the bleak desert, parched with thirst, and starved for some sort of genuine sustenance.

As this man reaches the ends of his physical limits his mind takes him into excitement. He races forward, only to find out forward is not forward at all.

He sees a pool of water to quench his thirst. No sooner has he used the last of his strength to lean down for a revitalizing drink does he discover that what he thought would give his Soul the meaning it requires, it is merely a mirage.

His mouth full of sand, he tries to rake it from his tongue with cracked and blistered hands, collapsing in defeat as he recognizes what he chased had been false. It was nothing at all.

To have purpose is to take each step with intention that is guided with greatness. Senses enriched, the purposeful man travels through the lush jungle, every nuance appreciated.

He does not go hungry, for in his appreciation he experiences the wonder of discovery in all life around him as he tastes fruit from the trees that his journey's path provides.

He does not go thirsty for he walks parallel to the water that gives all life. Resting as he sees fit, he drinks from this river.

Creativity

Creativity comes from the Universe and the Universe always provides.

One is not thinking outside the box when *the box* is thinking.

When the channel to Mother Source is open, it will flow into thoughts, transforming problems into solutions. It makes a way where before there was none.

It will shine the light of brilliance onto every man who wanders into the darkness of his cave of fears seeking the treasure that imagination so willingly offers.

Words create, so use your tongue wisely. For as creativity can be used to produce beauty, this very same magic can be misused, manipulated—creating ugliness that cannot be unseen.

Creativity is a basic need of being human, though is often overlooked, and reserved by those narrow in thought to the domain of the "artistic" types.

Creativity can seamlessly shift perspective through fluidity in psychic change.

It is the child seeing all of Noah's animals among the clouds in the arc of the sky.

Creativity sees each moment for what it is in the Great Reality— an opportunity for the expression of Love.

Creativity is freedom in its finest form. It gives flight to the bluebird in your heart. It is what convinces the lowly caterpillar that if it simply trusts the process, it will awaken as a monarch butterfly in all its splendor.

Creativity gives permission for the humble dream crawling along on the earth to take flight.

Anger

What is anger?

Anger is a mask. It wears itself either over the face of fear or the face of sadness. Anger is designed to prevent others from getting too close.

Anger's little brothers are frustration and irritability. Anger's cousins are anxiety and depression. It is revealing that anger is one letter away from danger—rage is when the angry mask is worn too often and for too long—the wearer comes to believe that he is a monster.

Anger can be frightening to experience and challenging to wield—a sword swung by wild emotion. Such a sword is the weapon carried by the man reluctant to shed his armor, uncertain of when the battle is ended, even when it is long over.

So take off your armor and quicken your pace, for the weight will slow your steps and make you weary.

This journey of life need not be a fight, for never did battle make peace. It is only through surrender that the abundant and ever-present peace may be realized.

Leadership

The true leader has nothing to prove to anyone, no reason to pick up weapons, and no reason to don the armor of ego.

He stands in his Truth—protected, protected by relationships forged in the fires of meaningful connection.

This leader knows his words are the only effective actions, and when aligned with his deeds, he will not stand alone.

He leads with his heart, and if he is criticized, it is only by the lost, cynical, and power-hungry. Because of this, he knows he will never be led astray, for his heart is never wrong.

The true leader has learned to always trust his gut, his mentors always asking him, "What does your gut say?"

As others see him lead from the front, alert in his Truth, they will follow the charge instinctively, as the same Truth is felt in each of their own gut.

You see, some are natural-born leaders but through the messiness of life, they lose faith in themselves—severing the connection of head and heart, casting the shadow of self-doubt through the hallways of authentic answers in the mansion of the mind.

So it is that doubt is cast out by the light illuminating the entryways to cavernous rooms where creation lies in wait.

So then how do we turn the lights back on? Like I said, we return to Self as we re-learn to trust our gut, and through this we reconnect to our Source of Power. The real Sorcerer is reborn, and the magic of life returns to our vision, and that is what is seen when others look into our eyes.

"But father," Ezekiel interjected, "How can a leader be sure of the direction in his commitment?"

"Now we come to intention, Ezekiel." Ishala continued on.

Intention

You cannot open a door with a closed fist. You reach out. You grasp. You turn it over.

So to live intentionally, one must move feet.

They say the road to hell is paved with good intentions. Conversely, the way to heaven is paved with clear intentions and strong actions.

Know where you want to go.

The Universe provides guides to show you that you're on course, encouraging you to keep moving. There are means of communicating with this Universe which are key to staying on course, and feeling this encouragement.

Let us speak of prayer and meditation.

Prayer

Abide by this prayer:

Higher Power, open my eyes
so that I may see the truth
that I am already surrounded by Light.
Teach me to keep my eyes open
so that I remain aware.
Show me how to open the eyes
of my brothers and sisters,
so that we may all bathe in your Love.
I trust you,
for I know the Universe provides.

Few know the meaning of praying without ceasing. It is to live in mindful compassion. This is the way, the truth, and the light embodied.

In practical terms, prayer is to use your mid-level of consciousness to set an intention with your higher level of consciousness, to override your lower level of consciousness.

Meditation

What of meditation then?

If prayer is to speak, then meditation is to listen.

Speak from the heart. Listen with the heart. So intention is to prayer as attention is to meditation.

Without meditation, I think, therefore I am. With meditation, *I am*, therefore I think.

Practicing meditation is akin to fiddling with the dial of an old transistor radio, initially only hearing static with the occasional sound of music.

As you get more in tune, the music becomes audible—then recognizable.

Once you've found your wavelength, you focus more with *listening* ears, and can soon identify lyrics.

Listen longer still and find the spaces between the lyrics, the gaps between notes. In that space resides the power of creation.

Meditation is not always smooth jazz or relaxing reggae; many are confused with this. Meditation is also loud death metal, and jolting EDM.

Meditation is not always sitting still. It can be a walk or even a sprint, but if you really want to know the Truth within you, be still and sit quietly. There you will find the necessity and rewards of *listening*.

Listening

Learn to listen for the lesson and find your guru in everything, everyone, and everywhere.

Listening is such a gift, for we all need to be heard.

The skilled listener can pick up on the softest tones, decode the muttered madness, and hear through the screams. Yes, the active listener can hear hurt and translate pain.

Listening opens a space for those challenged by speaking their needs.

Listening is a teacher; its education in understanding and connection.

Understanding

So let us speak of understanding.

To be understood is to be rescued from the Isle of Loneliness.

So then, as St. Francis wrote, it is better to understand than to be understood.

Understanding is without direction for the sage; however, for as he knows you, he knows himself; and as he knows himself, he knows you. Understanding opens doors to compassion, to forgiveness, to peace of mind and comfort of body.

"Speak to me more of the sage, father."

"To speak of the sage is to speak of wisdom, my son."

Wisdom

Wisdom asks the question: Who is it that's speaking? Is it my gut? Or is it my ego? Most men walk the earth with a broken interpreter.

Because of this, many poor decisions are made, even if the decision is to make no decision at all.

Wisdom knows it need not suffer needlessly.

Wise mind thinks with Source. Source knows the path.

Wisdom whispers and impulse yells, so listen carefully with your ear to the door. The whispers will lead your Spirit toward wakefulness.

Spiritual Awakening

The world is full of sleepwalkers; many can't see the light of day because they will not open their eyes.

I have learned that "Pain is the touchstone of Spiritual growth," so when you hear the expression—*eyes wide with pain*—you understand the deeper meaning. The awakened one sees the deeper meaning in the world around him, the world he is *in*, though is not *of*.

Many say, "Oh, I'm not a morning person," and this can be true, for many wake up slow—gaining momentum as they go about their day.

For Self to be fully alive, self must fully die. So to have a Spiritual awakening is to come to terms with the Great Reality, leaving the nightmare of hell, you now are living the dream of heaven.

"But what do we mean when we speak of spirituality, father?"

Ishala considered his words with care, then answered.

Spirituality

Spirituality connects us all. It is the awareness that if I hurt you, I hurt me. If I help me, I help you.

So do not just treat others how *you* wish to be treated. Of equal importance is to treat yourself the way you want *other people* to treat you.

I have heard that religion is to sit in church and think about fishing, whereas Spirituality is to be fishing and thinking of God. For the Spiritual man, everything under the heavens is his church and his place of worship within.

It is also said that religion is for people who don't want to go to hell, whereas Spirituality is for people who have already been there. And so, the Spiritual man is both wise and compassionate, knowing fully there is enough Love to go around.

If Love is your religion—true Love, then your religion is all inclusive.

The Spiritual man does not force his beliefs upon you. He lives by principles, so it is possible to be both religious and Spiritual.

The Spiritual man seeks Truth. Living inquiry, he asks questions to eliminate any agenda of ego and operate from integrity.

Integrity

But what is integrity?

Integrity is to walk the talk, leaving no need for masks. A person of integrity has no secret self; his principles unbreakable, he has no employer. His only superior is God.

Self-governed, he is truly a free man who lives in Truth. He does not need any persuasion or direction to do the right thing.

If a worldly boss asks him to do the wrong thing, it is impossible for the man with integrity to follow such an order.

And so it is that the man with integrity takes no orders, as his own house is in order.

The man in masks has many faces. He cannot be trusted. Insecure he behaves as a chameleon, blending in to survive.

Survival is not living. Look in the mirror. Take off your mask. To live you must be vulnerable.

"I confess, father, that this seems a difficult path to maintain throughout a lifetime." Ezekiel's brow furrowed in dismay.

"Then let us speak of perseverance, son."

Perseverance

Perseverance is to be beaten bloody in the ring, round after round after round—to the point of exhaustion, but somehow summoning the strength to get back in again to throw another punch—to take another hit.

It is to keep swimming even when it feels like you're going upstream, fighting a rapid current.

In the words of the Reverend Dr. Martin Luther King, Jr., "If you can't fly then run, if you can't run then walk, if you can't walk then crawl, but whatever you do you have to keep moving forward."

To persevere is to not quit before the next miracle, adhering to the words of Albert Einstein who said, "There are two ways to live your life. One is as though nothing is a miracle. The other is as though everything is a miracle." The person who sees everything as a miracle therefore will never quit.

Obstacles turn to building blocks, rising up so that barriers become stepping stones.

Perseverance beats the heart of the Spiritual giant.

Perseverance will always put one foot in front of the other, with the absolute understanding that dreams are not realized standing still.

The legs of the persevering are strong, their breathing deep and steady, oxygenating their mind and bodies.

The persevering one looks at a problem from every angle, sleepless nights spent in analysis, unable to rest until a solution is found, like a homicide detective continuing to search the landscape of evidence until the next truth presents itself.

Thinking

So what of thinking, then?

Thinking is a *doing*, so when we are *doing* thinking we are not *being*.

Thinking is manipulative, convincing you that you're present when you're not.

Constructively, thinking can bring you back to center, re-awakening you to the Present Moment.

Many of life's problems and all of its stress center in the mind. We learn to get out of our own way when we learn to think *non-thinking,* when we learn to watch our thoughts as a curious child watches a train cross over the tracks, seated in the back seat, watching through the window.

Thinking can come in layers. This is rare. Layered thinking can be your worst enemy or it can be your best friend—contingent on state of mind.

Do I think *problem* or do I think *solution*? Obsession is to think without ceasing. Presence is to pray without thinking.

Is my mind obstructed by the webbing of thinking, or is it a clear channel to my God?

Logic

Logic is a wonderful tool, but is oft overused.

Reason can pull emotion back to the center of wisdom, but without emotion pulling logic back to center, man loses the meaning of humanity.

Sure, problem-solving—no problem!

But to deprive yourself of empathy is to hold your breath surrounded by the fragrance of gardenia blooms.

Perspective & Flexibility

If I *have* to do something, the task at hand becomes a dreaded chore. If I *get* to do that very same task—I shift gears of cognition into the state of gratitude.

I travel lighter which means I travel farther.

We know that a glass half empty is a glass half full, is ultimately half a glass, so why not choose *fullness*?

Live in want. Live in contentment. Or simply live *simply*—your choice.

Anxiety

A nxiety is your buddy. Change your relationship with anxiety, and anxiety will change its relationship with you.

First it is a foe, and it fights back.

Embrace it openly, listen for the message it whispers in your ear, and both of you will part ways.

Like an indicator light on the dash, it shows us what isn't working. Ignore it and you eventually will break down—panic.

Use it as data and take corrective action, and you will travel smoothly again.

Fight your friend and become ever more agitated.

Wrestle and resist it, you will be battered and bruised, left fatigued and gasping for breath.

Obsession

Obsession is the background noise interfering with the sound of Presence.

Obsession is grabbing hold of a rock, then squeezing, and squeezing until your hand hurts. It is a defiant unwillingness to let go.

To obsess is to stalk a thought with another thought, and following that thought is another thought, ad infinitum.

The second thought looks much like the first. The third much like the second, though there are subtle differences.

Each stalker becomes slightly more aggressive than the last, for obsession is dangerous.

Rational thought is muffled by the clamorous demands of obsession.

Secrecy & Honesty

The secrets you decide to take to your grave will likely be the very secrets that take you to your grave.

By keeping our mouths closed we choose to stay sick. The remedy is Truth, for honesty is medicine for intimacy, which is the cure-all for loneliness. It is well known that *no man is an island.*

Secrets are the moat circling the castle walls, teeming with voracious alligators. The walls there—the shadow of our secret self, darkening our hearts that are hungry for light to beat purposefully again.

So speak what you fear to say and feel its hold lose its power over your heart and mind as it rolls across your tongue, for Truth is Freedom.

The web of lies will choke the life out of the butterfly, trapping its beautiful wings in place, surrendering its heart to ill fate.

"You mentioned a secret self?" Ezekiel asked with intrigue.

Secret Self

The secret self is the last wall separating a person from true vulnerability.

The shadow ceases its existence when surrounded by light. The shadow whispers secrets of freedom and control, but tells you that you can tell no one.

Projections of personal loss are part of the meal that feeds the secret self.

It fills its belly with an entrée of censorship, a side of doubt, with the aftertaste of anxiety in its mouth, and fueled by perfectionism. If you don't feed it, it won't grow.

It is silly that a man believes he is his own shadow, but I tell you, some cannot reconcile the difference, as they return to the same table to eat only to suffer food poisoning.

Self-Sabotage

This brings us to self-sabotage, which is a beast of many heads—all of them ugly to see.

One face of this monster is jealousy. The fear of being pushed out pushes out.

Another head you hope not to see is addiction. Freedom is scary when you have Stockholm syndrome. This is why the abused so often return home after having been away for some time. They come to rely on pain—this is the insanity of addiction.

The third head is arrogance; this head sits atop a long neck looking down on you, and because of this you find others to look down on; it is similar to the way bullies are born.

The fourth head is shame. It rolls its eyes in disapproval. "Who are you kidding? They see you. They know you don't deserve such an abundant life."

Self-sabotage is to set your own booby trap and then walk right into it.

Self-sabotage partners with denial, so you walk into oncoming traffic, color-blinded—red and green trade places. It is backward.

Be grateful for your fears, for they are your opportunities to take courage. When fears become opportunities, prepare for a growth spurt. For your reality changes and what was once considered intimidation is now merely considered new.

Communication

I'll talk of *talk.*

Communication is the bridge between true relationship.

Know that it is easier to build a new bridge than to rebuild it once it has been burnt, for then wreckage must be cleared away first. This is a costly and time-consuming effort, so build sturdy structures, and watch the weight of your words. Some words have no place on the bridge between you and your brother.

Communication by way of the written word is stifled without clear mind.

No peace until you know peace. The conflicted mind sends a mixed message.

How can you send your message if you cannot get quiet with yourself long enough to know what message it is you wish to send? Many fights are caused by this lack of pause.

With a silver tongue, you can tell anyone anything. Use tact and there will be no need for attack.

Read the words aloud and find no reason for defense. We do not shoot the messenger for doing what they believe is their job. If it is junk mail, do not let it stack up in your house creating disorganization, chaos, mess.

Remember, the weight of words on our hearts and minds is contingent on the meaning we assign to them. If we assign the meaning to be *mean*, we hurt ourselves.

We did not write these words, let us not assume mal-intent. So if you are not the person who wrote the words, why would you take them personally?

Always in awe of how his father took nothing personally, Ezekiel questioned, "Betrayal, is that not a personal message?"

Betrayal

Betrayal is the fracturing of trust, like a window pane that has had a stone thrown through it. The broken glass pieces of the relationship strewn about, its jagged edges sharp to the touch, cutting fingers as we try to pick up the pieces as blood drips from a broken heart.

It is a messy business, this destruction of property is.

The broken window allows the angst of nature to be blown inside.

Pride & Humility

Why do so many struggle with asking for help then?

Many confuse helplessness with helpfulness. For when we reach out with our arm and grab firmly ahold of another hand, does that not require a certain kind of strength?

Pride is a muscle over-used, to the point that all other muscles wither and atrophy.

Pride keeps a man driving in circles, rather than stopping and seeking direction. So it is really a waste of time and energy to let pride drive the vehicle.

To be right-sized is to not only live in accordance with your own strengths, but also with your weaknesses, well aware of the strength of others. It is a strength to admit weakness, a weakness to deny the strength of another.

Surrender—for to awaken, you must set aside everything you think you know. To let go of ego is the ultimate ask for help.

Free up your hands and embrace the Universe. Empty your mind and accept the Divine Wisdom that hangs silently in the air all around you.

"Please, speak more to me of the way to manifest dreams. I want to free my hands for the Universe's embrace, father."

Ishala smiled broadly. "You remember my 'Pay your dues' speech, don't you, Ezekiel?"

Paying Dues &
Manifesting Dreams

S low down. For as the tortoise beat out the hare, this human
race is a marathon, not a sprint.

This life is a garden, needing tending with regularity. Dig in
the abundant earth and plant your seeds. Water them patiently
and watch your plants grow.

As your plants grow, the picturesque color scheme becomes ever
more clear.

Pour your attention into each ambition as you would pour water
at the roots of each budding flower.

Do not drown the roots in a foolish attempt to make the flower
grow faster. This is the way that dreams die. Of course, not all
buds are destined to bloom.

Heartbreak

Heartbreak, true heartbreak, is never-ending Love that seems to have met its end. It is the separation of two Souls.

Sometimes Souls shine too bright together. They charge one another. They light up the world, teaching each other how to *really* feel again.

In touch with all of their feelings, the two converged Souls part ways, in pain but also in gratitude, thankful for each blessed moment shared. So this is the bitter sweetness we contract with in this life.

They say *to have loved and lost is better than to have never loved at all.* And so, we know this to be true, as two Spirits are enriched through their convergence, these Spirits do not lose their enrichment when they diverge.

The magic of True Love travels with each heart, for as it is broken in this way, there become two hearts—full of Light.

Remember, the Sun continues to give Light to the Moon, for even though they cannot be together, the Moon shines Light into darkness, carrying his Love. And this is why in heartbreak, it only *seems* as though Love has met its end. In all reality, this Love *is* never-ending, for you see, the Moon—*she never forgets*, always remembering the passion of the Sun.

Letting Go

Letting go is to stop desperately clinging to the root protruding from the embankment—and let the flow carry you—allowing nature to take you to new scenery.

There is an ease to this practice. The man that lives in the let-go is like a duck, his problems are water that beads and rolls off of his back.

It is the out breath, the release of control—that control stifling our life force, because the breath cannot be held indefinitely.

This illusion of control, this "self-will run riot" will lead a man to an early grave if left unchecked.

The philosophy of "Live in the Let-go" speaks wisdom—reminding you to go with the flow. Just make sure you are in the right river.

Letting go is understanding that all physical appearances are unstable, ever-changing, and ultimately temporary.

With arms full of worldly attachments, this man is grief, anger, and fear embodied as he obsessively exerts the effort to hold onto that which is not meant to be held.

Letting go is living in the wisdom of experience. This man need not worry about dropping anything, because he has learned *not* to pick up that which does not belong to him. As he ages, he realizes his peace. Each day understanding more and more that all of us are simply "passing through."

The man who lives in the *let-go* does not suffer less, he merely experiences it with a deep joyful appreciation for being with it, before he's met with its winter season.

Grief & Loss

Grief is a transformative process. Grief transforms through its stages—reaching resolution in acceptance.

Grief is part of your contract with being human. To have loved and lost is to have lived.

Grief transforms its carrier as well. Some say they lose a piece of themselves when they lose their beloved. While still others are enhanced, carrying memories in gratitude and living the learnings of those lost. It is on this path of loss that they find themselves.

Carrying the hurt will lead to collapse. Denying death does not change the reality that it is a most natural phase of life's cycle.

Some feel guilt if their hearts stop hurting as they learn to live again, as they learn to love again.

I ask of you, when I am gone: honor my memory. Celebrate my life. My death does not make you a victim. That story, son, is one not worth reading.

Death, though a time of grief for the human, is a time of rebirth for the Soul.

One dies more than once, and some never truly live. For rebirth to occur there must first be death.

To be awakened is to be reborn in each moment anew. As a caterpillar goes to sleep to wake as a butterfly, man too goes to sleep to wake his Spirit.

When a man lives awakened in Spirit, how can he die? His body no longer has purpose, so do not live in the remorse of this final departure Home.

I ask you to be happy for those who leave the ego with permanence in the pursuit of their Home.

Home is from where we came from and where we all at our core wish to return. We come from Love and we return to Love, for we are Love.

Return To Love

Ishala smiled and placed his hand on Ezekiel's. Ezekiel firmly squeezed his father's hand, and in that moment, Ishala, the Wonderful Counselor, returned Home.

Tears streamed down Ezekiel's cheeks, and as they did he smiled inwardly to himself, grateful for the final gift his father gave him.

As Ezekiel gave his father's hand that final squeeze, he looked out the window to see an enormous turkey vulture perched on the deck railing outside. The last breath left his father, and as it sighed away into the air, Ezekiel watched the big bird take flight. For some time, Ezekiel sat there in quiet reflection, peaceful tears rolling down his cheeks. Then he looked back outside, taking in the vibrancy of the lush green forest shimmering in the sunlight. As he took in the beautiful sight, a large blue butterfly flew up to the glass fluttering its wings. In his knowing, Ezekiel smiled.

Though he was deeply saddened, he was tremendously grateful. Ezekiel realized how special his father was and in that moment Ezekiel was filled with pride, proud to be the son of such a wonderful counselor, a man that lived a life of love and service with each word he spoke and each breath he took.

Ezekiel made an agreement with himself to sit quietly alone for some time, grieving the loss of his father while recording his wisdom, so that he might share it with the world.

As promised, Ezekiel carried his father's collected wisdom back to the people of Manasseh. Like his father, he sat down with them individually, creating a safe space in which to speak the language of the heart.

Though he passed on his father's wisdom to those with open ears, he also, just like his father, would listen with love as the people of Manasseh shared their pain with him. And through that sacred interaction they showed Ezekiel their wounds and he healed them. For just like Ishala, in Ezekiel's presence the people always felt seen and always understood.